Mama and Me and the Model T

Faye Gibbons
illustrated by Ted Rand

Morrow Junior Books
New York

Watercolors were used for the full-color illustrations.
The text type is 14.5-point Figural Book.

Published by Morrow Junior Books
a division of William Morrow and Company, Inc.
1350 Avenue of the Americas, New York, NY 10019
www.williammorrow.com

Printed in Singapore at Tien Wah Press.

3   5   7   9   10   8   6   4   2

Library of Congress Cataloging-in-Publication Data
Gibbons, Faye.
Mama and me and the Model T / Faye Gibbons; illustrated by Ted Rand.
p. cm.
Summary: When Mama gets behind the wheel of the new Model T that her husband just drove into the
yard of their Georgia mountain home, she proves that she can drive a car as well as the men of the family.
ISBN 0-688-15298-8 (trade)—ISBN 0-688-15299-6 (library)
[1. Automobiles—Fiction.   2. Sex roles—Fiction.   3. Mountain life—Georgia—Fiction.   4. Georgia—Fiction.]
I. Rand, Ted, ill.   II. Title.   PZ7.G33913Mam 1999   [E]—dc21   98-31518   CIP AC

For my friend Sandra L. Ballard,
who always believed in me
—F.G.

In memory of my mother, Martha,
who drove a Model T
—T.R.

It was fall in the Georgia mountains when my stepfather went to town. Mr. Long left early one morning when the leaves were turning to gold.

Mama and us five Searcy young'uns gathered in the yard with the seven Long kids to say good-bye. It was me Mr. Long winked at.

"Mandy girl," he said, "I'll be bringing a surprise when I come home today."

And he did.

We were setting the table for dinner when we heard
Put-put-pow! Rackety-put. Rackety-put-pow!

Us young'uns knew that only one thing could make
such a grand and glorious sound. "A motorcar!" said my
brother Larry Ray.

Sure enough, down the road came a Model T, chugging
along the pasture fence, scaring the mules and the cows.
It lurched into the yard, burping and hissing, and came to
a stop with a honk on the horn. *Urrrh-ru-gah!*

Earl Long gave out a whoop. "Papa bought a motorcar!"

Mary Lucy, the youngest Long, grabbed my hand tight and we hurried outside with the others. Cheering and laughing, all of us gathered around the car with the barking dogs.

"Who wants a ride in a Model T?" Mr. Long asked, climbing out of the car with a great big smile.

"Me!" us young'uns yelled together. We crowded into that motorcar—all us Searcy kids and all the Longs, one of the dogs, and two cats. Jimmy Long and my brother Robert perched on the running boards. Mama and Mr. Long could barely squeeze in. We were sitting on legs and standing on toes, poking elbows in ribs and noses in hair.

Mr. Long drove. We *rackety-putted* all around the farm.
We bounced and jiggled down to the spring. We rattled
by our cotton fields. We joggled around the barn and
splashed through the creek. At last we stopped at the
front porch.

"Now gather round, boys," Mr. Long said when we'd all piled out. "You'll be driving this motorcar someday. You girls step back."

"Cars are for boys," said Larry Ray.

He scrambled up with the other boys as Mr. Long told them what to push and what to pull and what to twist.

"Who remembers all that?" he asked when he turned the crank and the car roared to life.

"I do," said all the boys together.

"I do," said Mama and Kate Long and me along with them.

Mr. Long edged us girls aside. "Pay attention, boys, while I show you again. Men need to learn to drive."

"And girls don't," Kermit Long said. "Girls just ride."

Once again Mr. Long set the levers and turned the crank, and the Model T went *rackety-put, rackety-put.* "Any man can do it," he said.

Mama took off her apron and handed it to me. "Then so can any woman."

"Yes," said all us girls.

"No!" yelled the boys.

"Wait!" said Mr. Long, leaping to block her path. But Mama was too quick for him. She dodged around his reaching hands and sprang into the motorcar.

Rackety-put-put-Put!

"Get in the house, young'uns!" Mr. Long yelled, grabbing Mary Lucy and Larry Ray.

But I didn't go. I dropped Mama's apron and jumped into the motorcar with her. "We'll show 'em," I said.

Mama gave a little wave and a great big smile. The engine roared and the Model T jolted backward across the yard.

"Oh my!" Mama cried, and the car lunged into the clothesline.

Clangabang-clangabang-pow!!

"Push that left pedal!" I screamed. Mama did—and the car leaped forward, dragging the clothesline behind. We tore across the yard, cutting through a flower bed and bouncing over the woodpile. *Clangabang-clangabang-pow!*

Thumpety-thump!
Bonkety-bonk!

We scraped under the branches of the pear tree and fruit rained down on us. We bobbed across a stump at the edge of the yard and ran over a crape myrtle bush. When we clipped a scarecrow in the garden, its hat landed on my head.

Around the barn we zoomed, once, twice, and then a third time. Mama flattened a pine sapling before tearing through the pasture fence and shimmying over a hill.

Mama turned the steering wheel, and the car swung around in a wide half circle. She yelled, "I'm learning!"

Urrrh-ru-gah!

"You sure are, Mama," I yelled back. "But the road's over there."

"So it is," Mama said, turning again and bumping across a ditch.

When at last we got to the road, somehow Mama stayed mostly on it. "Guess we showed them who can drive a car," she shouted.

"So let's go home," I answered.

As we pulled into the yard, we saw Mr. Long and a string of Searcy and Long young'uns running to meet us. Mama stopped the car with a *pow* and one long *urrrh-ru-gah!* Then we stepped out.

POW!
Urrrh-ru-gah!

"This motorcar has a mind of its own," Mama said.
"It's not the only one," Mr. Long replied. He took a
deep breath and mopped his face with a handkerchief.
Then he smiled at Mama and all us young'uns. "I guess,"
he said slowly, "this Model T belongs to all of us."

And it did.